Library Media Center
Longwood Elementary School
30W240 WITHDRAWN
Naperville, IL 60563

W9-BPL-026

A WATER SNAKE'S YEAR

A
Water Snake's
Year

by
DORIS GOVE

illustrated by
BEVERLY DUNCAN

ATHENEUM   1991   NEW YORK

Library Media Center
Longwood Elementary School
30W240 Bruce Lane
Naperville, IL 60563

For Jeff Mellor, who used to be afraid of snakes —D.G.

For Megan & Stuart —B.K.D.

Great Smoky Mountains National Park Tennessee — to Knoxville — to Gatlinburg — Little River — Little River — Middle Prong

Text copyright © 1991 by Doris Gove
Illustrations copyright © 1991 by Beverly Duncan

All rights reserved. No part of this book may be reproduced or transmitted in any form or by any means, electronic or mechanical, including photocopying, recording, or by any information storage and retrieval system, without permission in writing from the publisher.

Atheneum
Macmillan Publishing Company
866 Third Avenue
New York, NY 10022

Collier Macmillan Canada, Inc.
1200 Eglinton Avenue East
Suite 200
Don Mills, Ontario M3C 3N1

FIRST EDITION

LIBRARY OF CONGRESS CATALOGING-IN-PUBLICATION DATA

Gove, Doris.
  A water snake's year / by Doris Gove; illustrated by Beverly Duncan.—1st ed.   p.   cm.
  SUMMARY: Presents a year in the life of a female water snake, resident of Great Smoky Mountains National Park.
  ISBN 0-689-31597-X
  1. Snakes—Juvenile literature. [1. Snakes.] I. Duncan, Beverly, 1947–   ill.   II. Title.
QL666.O6G615   1991   597.96—dc20

Printed in Hong Kong by South China Printing Company (1988) Ltd.   1 2 3 4 5 6 7 8 9 10

The water snake lay tightly coiled under a massive rock. She was deep enough in the ground that she would not freeze, but her body was stiff and wrinkled—so stiff that it seemed that she would break if forced to straighten out. Her heart beat once or twice a minute, and her thick blood carried just enough food and oxygen to keep her alive.

She breathed only a few times a day. She never changed her position, though if a warm spell melted the snow high above her for more than a week, her coils loosened a bit.

The water snake lived on the Tennessee side of the Great Smoky Mountains National Park, near the Middle Prong of the Little River. She was born there and never wandered far from home. Now in her sixth winter, she was two and one-half feet long. Her back was dark brown with chestnut red markings. Her head was almost black, and her belly had red half-moon spots on a yellow background. Like all water snakes, she had no fangs or venom, but she had strong jaws for catching fish and frogs.

Each fall she crept down a narrow crack beside this rock and, with the last of the year's sun energy, pushed herself far into the earth. Then leaves fell into the crack as first the nights and then the days got too cold for snakes to be out.

October, November. Rain fell and flattened the leaves against her rock.

December, January. Snow covered the leaves. Chickadees darted from tree to tree, calling to each other as they looked for seeds in pinecones. Below the ground, the snake lay still.

February. A warm thaw and breezes of spring air. Tiny frogs started singing.

March. Warm air; sunny days. White bloodroot and hepatica blossomed above the brown leaves, and a few early bees visited them. Gray-green flowers covered the ends of elm twigs and wiggled in the smallest breeze, scattering their pollen. The frogs sang every night.

April. Finally the earth warmth began to seep through the dirt above the hibernating chamber. The snake's heart rate doubled, then tripled, and her body pressed against the dirt walls. But still the nights were cold enough to take away the days' warmth.

One day the snake started pushing with her nose until she found a soft spot. Her head moved up through the dirt and the wet leaves as her body uncoiled below. She rested and crawled, rested and crawled, until her nose and eyes came out into the April sun, so bright it hurt. Her tongue flicked out and sampled the air, slowly at first, then faster. Leaves, damp earth, fresh water; all safe and normal smells. She felt the rhythm of the stream in the distance—a rhythm of water running smooth, swirling, falling, flowing, and rushing through rocky gaps.

She rested for an hour, her head like a curled oak leaf, her tail still in the hibernation chamber.

Then it was afternoon, starting to get cool again. She pulled herself out, slid under a nearby log, and slept.

The sun had been up for several hours when she woke up the next day. She was warm enough to move, but not warm enough to move fast. She needed more energy to be able to escape predators and to catch fish. She crossed a sunny patch of leaves, splashed into icy-cold water, and swam to her sunning rock, where she could start getting warm.

She pushed her head against the warm rock while her body swam forward with big S-shaped curves. Water tumbled and splashed around her. As soon as her head was dry, she lifted another part of her body onto the rock but held it up so that the water rolled off her scales into the water instead of onto the rock. She held that part of her body away from the rock until it was dry and then slid it above the waterline on the rock. This way no telltale splashes would be left on the rock to show a hungry predator where a snake might be sunning.

The sun dried her scales to a dusty gray brown just like the rock color. Her rock was in the middle of the stream, far enough away from the tall trees on the bank that the sun shone on it most of the day. Round gray lichens made a pattern on the rock that gave her good camouflage even when she was crawling up the side. There were hundreds of rocks in the stream, all colors, shapes, and sizes, and though the snake was out in the open, she was hard to see.

Tiny leaves fluttered over her head, water sparkled all around, and once in a while a bird swooped past, dipping its wings almost into the water. On one side of her rock, smooth water reflected the green and brown of the trees. Water striders darted back and forth, throwing golden shadows larger than themselves on the rocky streambed.

The water snake flicked her tongue to test the air for danger, such as the smell of a weasel or a raccoon. Then she moved her head down the side of the rock, flicking her tongue every inch or so.

Her body followed her head like a train following an engine, all along the same path. She moved so slowly that the hungry hawk flying overhead did not see her. She took several deep breaths and dived into the cold water.

As her back got wet, the red and brown pattern of her scales became visible, but quickly disappeared against the pattern of stream rocks and pebbles. She carried enough sun warmth in her body for a fishing trip. At the bottom of the stream, she flattened out and glided over and between the rocks, flicking her tongue the whole time. She moved upstream. Sometimes her tongue touched the rocks; sometimes it just tested the water flowing by.

She smelled a fish—somewhere up ahead. She could not see it, but she knew that it was just on the other side of a slippery rock. She pushed off with her strong rib muscles and slid around the rock. When she smelled that the fish was close, she opened her mouth wide and moved her head back and forth as she shot forward. The fish felt ripples in the water and tried to flip out of the way, but the snake's mouth closed down on its tail, and her jaws and backward-pointing teeth held it tight.

She carried the fish to a shady secret place on the bank. It flopped as she turned it bit by bit until it faced down her throat. She swallowed it by moving one side of her jaw and then the other—almost like walking it into her mouth. When the fish tail, still wiggling, disappeared, she moved her neck and body to push the fish to her stomach, about one-third of the way down her body.

Then she stretched her jaws in a huge pink yawn and swam back to her sunning rock.

The fishing was good in the Middle Prong. As the snake moved upstream, flicking her tongue, she approached schools of minnows. Healthy fish usually dashed away, but fish that were sick or wounded were slower. Sometimes she caught one fish, held it in her jaws, and lunged after another. Then she took them to the bank and swallowed them, one after the other.

She fished every day and started to get fat. But one morning, as she swam to the sunning rock, she felt slow and tired. After a few minutes of sunning, she slid into the water and moved toward a big, flat rock between the stream and some tall weeds.

She flicked her tongue rapidly as she moved into the darkness under the flat rock. She could smell that other water snakes had been there, and she knew from the scent whether they were male or female, large or small, from her stream or from another stream. She also smelled a garter snake and a deer mouse.

The smell of weasel was around, but it was old.

The snake's eyes were milky white, and many scales on her back and sides were torn. Some ticks had burrowed underneath her scales, and they hurt.

She still needed sun warmth, but she got it by creeping silently into the weeds and flattening herself against the warm side of a rock. Some afternoons only her head and upper third of her body came out into the sun; the rest of her body was wedged in a crack, ready for a quick, silent retreat from danger.

For six days she waited. She crawled into the weeds for an hour a day to get some sun, but otherwise she just rested in the cool darkness.

Then she began to itch. Her chin and nose itched the most, and she bent her head down toward the rough ground and rubbed. The scales of her lips peeled back first, then the big, curved scales of her head, then the round eye scales.

Next came the long job of pulling the whole skin off inside out. If the skin broke, the little shreds would be hard to get off later. And she had to work quietly, since it would be almost impossible to escape from a predator while shedding. She was tired—she hadn't eaten for a while and had not soaked up as much sun energy as she needed.

The old skin on her body was damp and stretchy, but the chin and head parts dried off. She pushed her head through a large crack in the rock where the rough surface caught the bits of loose skin. She squeezed her body through, moving first one side, then the other, and the scales peeled away. She peeled four or five rows of scales, then rested, then started again.

When the skin was off, right down to the tip of her tail, she crawled out into the hot, noonday sun, looking like a new snake with shiny scales and red patterns on her back. She moved down to the stream, slid her mouth into the water, and drank several clear, cold gulps.

The old skin lay inside out, twisted around stones and twigs. It was dry and empty except for the ticks that were trapped inside.

She lay in the warm sun for a long time one May morning— long enough to soak up energy for several fishing trips. But today was a day for mating. All the snakes along the stream recognized the signs: The air and water had reached the right temperatures; the sun rose early enough to make a long day; and the air had a warm, earthy smell.

When she slipped off her rock, she stayed on the surface of the water and swam across the stream toward some bushes and wildflowers.

She left the water and pushed through moss and bluets, pressing her body against the sides of rocks. She headed upstream along the edge of a dark grove of hemlocks and rhododendrons. Her scales left a scent trail on the rocks and plants that would tell other snakes she had been there, which way she was going, and when. Other snakes would also know she was a female and ready for mating.

She moved along, flicking her tongue at the ground. Other water snakes moving out from their parts of the stream crossed her trail and turned upstream to follow it. Three male snakes, smaller and darker than she was, caught up with her and flicked their tongues along her back. She crawled faster and the males hurried to keep up, pushing against each other.

When she came to a sunny patch where the leaves were dry and warm, she stopped. The male snakes clustered around her, each trying to slide under or over closer ones. The largest, strongest one finally succeeded in pushing the others away without getting pushed away himself. He lined his body up against hers from head to tail and pushed down on her neck with his chin, moving his head in little jerks and flicking his tongue. The other snakes tried to push them apart as he slid his tail under hers.

The two snakes lay together for about half an hour. The other males continued to push and jostle.

Suddenly she twisted her body to one side and slid over the backs of the other snakes. She turned toward the stream, dashed to the water, and rode downstream on the current to her sunning rock.

July. Cicadas whined in the tops of the trees, and the midafternoon sun was so hot that it just took a few minutes of sunning to be ready for fishing.

A dragonfly skimmed across a still pool, dipping her abdomen into the water to lay eggs one at a time. When she came to the running water, she flew up, circled in the air, and came down to the calm pool for another egg-laying pass.

It hadn't rained for days. The woods were dry and the ground was hard. The sunning rock stuck much farther out of the water because the stream was low, and the snake sometimes used a smaller rock nearby.

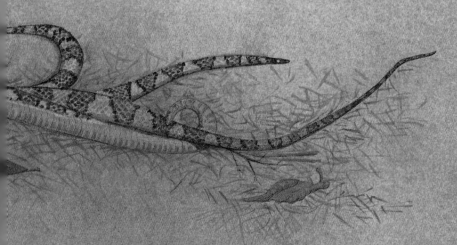

The sky wasn't blue; it wasn't gray. It was just something in between. The air sat heavy and still, and leaves hung down from their branches.

But slowly, almost unnoticeably, the air started to move with a low hushing noise. At the tops of the trees, the leaves started twisting back and forth. Lower leaves took up the motion, then leaves on the bushes, then the bluets by the water's edge danced back and forth. This new air was cool as it moved through the forest, always in the same direction, like a great, cool beast exhaling.

Far away, just barely louder than the wind, thunder rumbled. The snake felt the sudden lightness of the air and the distant vibrations. She drew her coils a little tighter and watched the leaves.

The sky turned dark gray and the wind became stronger. Lightning zigzagged from the clouds and thunder shook the earth. The first few raindrops fell and left walnut-sized blotches on the warm rocks. One drop hit the snake on the back and she jerked away from it. Then another, and finally a bunch of drops that made the wet spots on her rock grow together. She slid down into the water with no attempt to hide her movement.

The rain came stronger and stronger, first making craters on the water surface, and then forming a solid mass of small waves that were pushed by the wind. The snake was flat against the bottom of the stream, partly under one rock where the current was slow. She could feel the thunder.

The rain settled into a steady downpour as the lightning and thunder moved on over the mountain. Water formed crooked fingers rushing to the big stream, and waterfalls appeared on mossy rocks. The snake raised the front part of her body every ten minutes or so to breathe, but as soon as she felt rain on her head, she slipped back down to safety on the rocky bottom.

It rained hard for two hours. Then it became softer, like a whispering on the leaves, and the dark gray clouds turned white and started to break apart, showing a blue as bright as the green of the newly washed trees. The snake was cold and slow; she needed sun.

She swam toward the sunning rock. But a strong current of rushing cold water swept her right over it. Her familiar, comfortable spot on top was covered by floodwater that tumbled down from the tops and sides of the mountains. She turned back toward the bank and her shedding rock, but the current pulled her toward the middle again. She dived under the brown, frothy surface; even down there the water moved so fast that she couldn't wedge herself between rocks.

Just as she came up, the current swept her around a bend in the stream that had been the downstream boundary of her fishing range. Above that curve, she knew all the rocks and logs that made good hiding places, both in and out of the water. She knew which bottom rocks might shelter a juicy minnow. She knew which rocks were sunny in the morning and which were sunny in the afternoon. Now she was in a strange place and still rushing along.

Branches and leaves rode the current with her. She wrapped part of her body around a large branch and stopped trying to escape the current. She needed to save energy.

The snake and her branch slowed down as their stream met another at a deep pool surrounded by boulders. The water smelled different and strange. More branches met them and tangled together; a raft formed and turned completely around before drifting down the river. The snake crawled up on the raft and began to dry out and absorb sun warmth. The raft started moving fast again, down over standing waves and rapid channels between boulders.

The jagged end of one branch caught on a tree trunk that hung out from the bank, and the raft twisted around slowly as the water rushed on underneath. The snake crawled onto the trunk while the branches of her raft broke off one by one and continued down the river.

It was getting dark. She crept down the tree trunk and found a hole in the dirt at the base. She flicked her tongue around the hole for a long time and then slid into the darkness. Other snakes had used this hole, but none bothered her that night.

In the morning she crawled out to a sunny patch on the trunk and lay tense and alert while her body warmed up. A mosquito pierced a soft place between her scales and got an abdomen full of bright red snake blood.

The floodwaters had gone down and the water moved quietly under her. The morning sun burned the mist off the river. Sun warmth flowed through the snake's body.

There was a sudden movement upstream, and the snake twisted her head around, ready to jump to the safety of the water. Two people floated toward her in black inner tubes, kicking and splashing. The snake dived just as the inner tubes bobbed under her tree trunk. Both inner tubes flipped over, arms and legs crashed through the water, and the snake plunged out of sight and felt around for an underwater hiding rock. The people came up sputtering, and the inner tubes bounced away downstream.

The snake came up for a quick breath and then returned to the bottom. She turned upstream and moved around unfamiliar rocks, testing the water with her tongue.

She noticed a new underwater smell—like something she might eat, but very strange. She moved toward the smell and came to a muddy part of the stream bottom with tangled roots of water plants. Brown, rotted strands from the plants fluttered in the slow current. The smell became stronger.

A hellbender, a giant salamander, fluttered in the water weeds. It was mudbrown and had a flat head, tiny brown eyes, and ragged folds of skin along its sides. It stood up on the tips of its toes and swayed back and forth. The snake came close and touched the hellbender with her tongue. The hellbender rose a little higher on its toes and fluttered faster. It was three or four times as big around as the snake and almost half as long.

The snake swam out of the tangle of weeds and turned upstream again. Sometimes the water smelled right and sometimes it smelled wrong.

She slowly made her way back to the large pool where the two streams came together. She went from bank to bank, testing the water with her tongue. Even though she could smell fish and the clean forest soils that she was used to, it just wasn't quite right. She crossed the pool.

Suddenly the water smelled right and she began to hurry. Trees shaded the stream, and the water was cool, clean, and familiar. She swam around the broad curve and approached her own part of the stream.

She struck out straight through the water, not flicking her tongue, swimming as fast as she could against the current. She reached the base of her sunning rock and carefully raised her head until it was dry and then raised parts of her body a few inches at a time. The floodwaters had left twigs and brown leaves on her rock, which helped her climb and made her camouflage almost perfect once she was all curled on top.

August. The snake had several days of peaceful weather and good fishing. She got longer and heavier; pulling up onto her sunning rock was beginning to be difficult. She shed her skin again.

One morning, after the sun rose high above the tall hemlock trees, the snake curled up on her sunning rock, got warm, and then swam to the bank. She crawled up a small ridge and down the other side, flicking her tongue. Every once in a while she stopped with her head held high for several seconds, then she flicked her tongue and continued, pushing forward against rocks and logs.

She came to a park trail—an open place with hard ground and rocks and nothing to hide under. Her tongue picked up smells of danger, smells of people and big animals, but they didn't seem to be fresh smells, so she moved across the trail. Half of her body was out of sight on the other side when two boys came running down the trail. She felt the vibrations from their feet and dashed into the safety of some thick ferns and bushes.

The snake waited until she felt no more footsteps and the smell of humans faded. Then she crawled through the rhododendron, flicking her tongue and pressing close to rocks and trees.

Soon she came to an open area with tall grass that was matted down. Small animals had made tunnels in the grass, and she followed these twisting tunnels until she reached the edge of a pond. Her tongue picked up a delicious frog smell as she moved silently along the pond bank. Every few inches she stopped with her head high. She looked like a brown stick.

The frog smell grew fresh and strong. The snake lowered her head so her chin slid along the ground. She flicked her tongue fast with no up-and-down movements that might catch the frog's attention. She didn't have to open her mouth to flick her tongue; a little hole at the front of her jaws was just big enough to let the tongue out.

Inch by inch the snake got closer to the frog, and then she started to pull coils of her body forward so she could strike. But suddenly a shadow passed over the bank, and the frog exploded out of the tall grass, squeaked a loud *eeep*, and plopped into the pond. Five other frogs jumped at the same time, and underwater clouds rose where they buried themselves in the mud.

The little green heron that had made the shadow turned in the air and landed in shallow water at the other end of the pond. It stretched its neck and then settled down, its sharp beak pointing at the water, waiting for fish or frogs to swim by.

The snake stayed in her spot for a long time, until she was as warm as she ever got on her sunning rock. The she slipped into the water and swam toward a different part of the bank.

She crawled out in some thick reeds and smelled frog again. This one was bigger, and she stalked until she was within striking distance. She gathered her body up in tight coils and sprang forward with her mouth wide open. The frog leaped as soon as it saw the movement of the snake, but its *eeep* was cut short as the snake's jaws clamped around its middle. They fell into the pond together and splashed around.

The snake wound her tail up onto the bank and pulled the frog backward into the reeds. She held it in her mouth, and its kicking became weaker.

It took a long time to get her mouth around the frog's head and front legs. She rested often, lying still in the cover of the reeds, with two long, slender frog legs sticking out of her mouth. When the knobby frog toes disappeared down her throat, she opened her mouth in a wide yawn and flicked her tongue to test for danger. The skin over her full stomach was so stretched that each scale was separated from the others.

She moved from the reeds to the thick grass of the bank and coiled up. Afternoon sun dappled the ground around her, warming her body and giving her good camouflage protection. She rested her chin on her back and watched.

That night she slept under a fallen tree trunk. The sun was already high when she crawled out the next morning, and she stretched along the brown tree bark. After a couple of days of resting and sunning, her stomach returned to its normal size, but the rest of her body was fatter. She caught another big frog and rested again.

After dark a raccoon snuffled around her hiding place under a fallen pine tree. She flattened her body and squeezed back into a crack between the trunk and the ground. The raccoon's nose didn't fit under the log at first, but it reached in with its claws. The snake pulled back even more and shifted one coil of her body behind a rock as the raccoon started digging.

Soon the raccoon got its nose and one paw under the tree trunk, and it reached in and scratched the snake. She shifted again just out of reach of the sharp claws. The raccoon couldn't dig any deeper because of the rocks, so it left. The snake stayed stiff and squeezed until morning.

Late August. The snake crawled back home to her familiar stream and sunning rock. Her body dragged and she wasn't hungry. She spent a lot of time hiding under logs or rocks, and the rest of the time, she lay in the sun on the banks.

One morning, she moved away from the stream and crawled to a small clearing surrounded by thick rhododendrons and dog-hobble. She flicked her tongue along the ground, in the leaves, and up in the air as she circled the clearing.

Then she raised her tail so that her vent was lifted off the ground and pushed out a brown, roundish lump. It was shiny and sticky, and as it settled onto a leaf, two more appeared. The snake lowered her tail and rested.

The first lump changed its shape and a tiny brown, gray, and red head popped out of one side. The baby flicked its tongue so fast that it looked like a blur. Heads came out of the other two lumps, also flicking their tongues. A breeze made some nearby rhododendron leaves dance, and all three heads drew back into the lumps.

The snake moved across the clearing, raised her tail, and deposited four more little brown lumps. The firstborn baby stretched its head and began to unravel its skinny body. The lump became stuck to a leaf that was heavier than the baby snake, and when the snake was almost completely out, it seemed to be stuck, too. It pulled and pulled, and finally snapped the umbilical stalk that connected it to the inside of the brown membrane. The little snake tumbled sideways and lay there for a moment, flicking its tongue. Then it darted out of sight under some leaves.

The other babies came out, and they also disappeared. The mother snake crawled and rested, crawled and rested, depositing two or three brown lumps each time.

She produced forty-two lumps. Five were born dead, and three were not strong enough to break out of the membrane, which dried and hardened.

The mother snake crawled straight to the stream and swam to her sunning rock. She was tired, but her body had become so thin that climbing up was easy. She rested her chin on her back and felt the rhythm of the stream.

The babies scattered in all directions from the clearing. Each one found a rough rock or piece of bark and shed its first, lacy skin. One baby crawled in front of a silent toad and got snapped up and swallowed.

Another baby met an iridescent blue beetle and pulled back into a strike coil, ready for battle. The beetle scuttled away. A third baby snake found a little brown salamander under a wet leaf and ate it.

Early September. The air grew crisp and cool, and the snake had to lie in the sun for a long time before she could fish. But she was hungry. As soon as she could each morning, she dived into the clear, cold water and searched, moving slowly upstream until her tongue picked up fish smell. Fish were hard to find now, but the ones she did catch had plenty of fat stored for winter. The snake's hollow body started to get round again.

The cold nights made it dangerous to be away from safe hiding places, because a cold snake cannot move fast enough to escape from predators that also need to get fat for the winter. But the snake managed to be under cover whenever the coolness slowed her down.

Late September. Poplar and birch leaves started falling. They carpeted patches of still water, and the snake could use these leaf covers to come up for air without being seen.

A cold rain fell for two days, and the snake hid under a log. Late one afternoon a black bear crashed through the huckleberry bushes, moving its head from side to side, plucking ripe berries.

The next day the snake came out for an hour of sun. The day after that was warmer, and she sunned for several hours on the log. She did not try to fish—the water was much colder after the rain, and the nights were so cold now that she might not be able to digest any fish she caught.

Early October. Sunny and warm. Red squirrels squawked and chattered, chasing each other and leaping from branch to branch. Acorns, buckeyes, and hickory nuts fell, some hitting lower branches and bouncing far away from their parent trees.

The snake crawled off a warm tree trunk and turned away from the stream. She moved slowly and pressed her body against rocks and logs. Dry leaves had piled up, but she moved with almost no rustling. She flicked her tongue along the ground and moved her head from side to side. The smells of the rocks, the plants, and the soil were her map.

Chipmunks had been burrowing around her hibernation rock, and the dirt was soft. The snake poked around in three holes before choosing one and sliding her body down, bit by bit, until her tail slid out of sight.

Underneath the great rock, about two feet underground, she used the sun energy in her body to push against the walls and make the space a little bigger. Then she curled up, tight and wrinkled, as her heart rate slowed and her sun warmth seeped out into the earth.

INDEX